# THE PERFECT WIZARD

## Hans Christian Andersen

"Now," said the queen, "you must tell us
a fairy tale. And be sure it is both profound and instructive."
"But," added the king, "funny at the same time."

—from THE FLYING TRUNK

# THE PERFECT WIZARD

# Hans Christian Andersen

BY JANE YOLEN

ILLUSTRATED BY DENNIS NOLAN

DUTTON CHILDREN'S BOOKS / NEW YORK

*Now I want to tell you a story I first heard
when I was a little boy. Every time I have remembered that story,
it seemed to me to be even more beautiful. That's because stories,
like people, improve with age. Isn't that a blessing?*

—*from* WHAT FATHER DOES IS ALWAYS RIGHT

*To Ann K. Beneduce, mentor and friend*
—J . Y .


*To my grandson, Jamie*
—D . N .

---

Text copyright © 2004 by Jane Yolen

Illustrations copyright © 2004 by Dennis Nolan

All rights reserved.

*Library of Congress Cataloging-in-Publication Data*

Yolen, Jane.

The perfect wizard: Hans Christian Andersen / by Jane Yolen; illustrated by Dennis Nolan.—1st ed.

p.  cm.

Summary: A biography of the famous Danish writer of fairy tales,

interspersed with excerpts from his stories. Includes bibliographical references (p.  ).

ISBN 0-525-46955-9

1. Andersen, H.C. (Hans Christian), 1805-1875—Juvenile literature.  2. Authors, Danish—19th century—Biography—

Juvenile literature. [1. Andersen, H.C. (Hans Christian), 1805-1875.  2. Authors, Danish.]  I. Nolan, Dennis, date, ill.  II. Title.

PT8119.Y65  2004     839.8'136—dc22     2003055717

Published in the United States by Dutton Children's Books,

a division of Penguin Young Readers Group

345 Hudson Street, New York, New York 10014

www.penguin.com/youngreaders

Designed by Heather Wood

Manufactured in China

First Edition

3   5   7   9   10   8   6   4   2

**AUTHOR'S NOTE** * *I have retold the passages from Andersen's stories in this book, using as my template several different translations for my retellings—especially the Bredsdorff, Haugaard, and Le Gallienne translations mentioned below. A few of the many books I consulted are:*

Andersen, Hans Christian. *The Fairy Tale of My Life.* New York: The British Book Centre, 1954.

Ardizzone, Edward. *Ardizzone's Hans Andersen.* New York: Atheneum, 1978.

Bredsdorff, Elias. *Hans Christian Andersen: Eighty Fairy Tales.* New York: Pantheon Books, 1976.

Bredsdorff, Elias. *Hans Christian Andersen: The Story of His Life and Work.* New York: Charles Scribner & Sons, 1975.

Conroy, Patricia L., and Sven H. Rossel. *The Diaries of Hans Christian Andersen.* Seattle: University of Washington Press, 1990.

Haugaard, Erik. *Hans Christian Andersen: His Classic Fairy Tales.* Garden City, New York: Doubleday & Company, 1976.

Haugaard, Erik Christian. *Hans Christian Andersen: The Complete Fairy Tales and Stories.* Garden City, New York: Doubleday & Company, 1974.

Le Gallienne, Eva. *Seven Tales by H. C. Andersen.* New York: Harper & Row Publishers, 1959.

"This poet who sang in prose so that
not only animals, plants, and stones listened and were moved,
but toys came to life, goblins and elves became real, those horrible schoolbooks
seemed poetry; why, he squeezed the whole geography of Denmark
into four pages—he was a perfect wizard."
—AUGUST STRINDBERG

*"Andersen wrote more self-portraits than Rembrandt ever painted."*
—A DANISH CRITIC

*"I am an extraordinary personage. From me springs poetry,
descriptions of people who have never lived and yet are somehow more
amazingly alive than those who actually walk about on two legs."*

—from THE PEN AND THE INKWELL

ONCE UPON A TIME, a baby was born on a bed that was made from a coffin platform. The bed still had the black borders of cloth at the bottom. Life and death both sleeping together.

That baby was the great fairy-tale writer Hans Christian Andersen.

Or at least such was the story he told.

It was as much a fairy tale as any he ever made up.

*Once there was a man well acquainted with fairy tales.*
*In fact, they used to come knocking at his door.*
—*from* "THE WILL-O'-THE-WISPS ARE IN TOWN,"
SAID THE BOG WITCH

In fact Hans was born, on April 2, 1805, in an ordinary bed. He lived for twelve years with his parents in a tiny one-room house in Odense, a city in Denmark. A lanky child with white-gold hair, Hans was very homely, even by his own account.

His parents were terribly poor. His father was a shoemaker and his mother a washer-woman.

He had an older half sister he hardly knew.

His father's father was quite mad. He would wander into the woods and return singing loudly, beech leaves and garlands of flowers plaited in his hair.

His father's mother incessantly told lies.

Hans told lies, too. About his past life. About his present life.

He called them fairy tales.

"My life is a beautiful fairy tale," he wrote in his autobiography, "rich and happy."

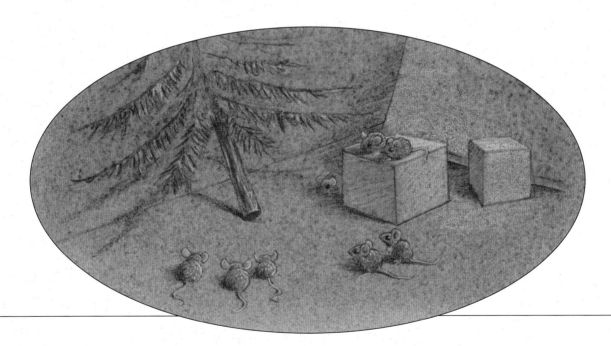

*"What marvelous stories you tell," cried the little mice.*
*They came back the following night with four of their mice friends,*
*all of whom wanted the tree to tell stories. And the more stories she told,*
*the better she remembered everything . . .*

—*from* THE FIR TREE

Hans grew up in a one-room house that was almost completely taken up by his father's shoemaker's bench, his parents' bed, and the couch on which little Hans slept.

Often he sat in the tiny courtyard of his house under a tent made from his mother's apron. The apron stretched from a wall of the house to a broom handle. There he would stare out at the solitary gooseberry bush, daydreaming and thinking of stories. There he made puppets and also spent time cutting out clothing for his dolls.

*"You want your puppets brought to life," he said.*
*"You want them to turn into real live actors,*
*and to be their manager. Then you*
*would be completely happy."*

—*from* THE PUPPET-SHOW MAN

From his mother—who could not read—Hans learned folklore and superstitions: about how spring water gathered at Midsummer Eve held great power; about sticking sprigs of Saint-John's-wort into the chinks of roof beams and checking which way they grew to see if he would have a long life; about how crossing running water would keep you safe from trolls.

From his father he learned about books. Every night his father would read aloud from *The Arabian Nights* or from books of plays that sat on a shelf over the cobbler's bench.

His father also made him a toy theater which had a cord that, when pulled, changed pictures within the box.

Though Hans remained superstitious for the rest of his life, it was his father's love of books and stories, of poetry and plays, that was to make the greatest lasting impression on him.

*Once there was a prince who had a library*
*that was greater than anyone in the world ever had,*
*either before him or since.*

—*from* THE GARDEN OF EDEN

Hans went to several schools. At the first school, the teacher hit him with a birch rod for making a mistake. Hans simply picked up his books and went home, never to return to that school.

By the third school, he was the teacher's pet, receiving cakes and flowers from the man. But the other children did not like Hans. He had a habit of making up stories in which he always played the hero.

When he told one little girl he was a nobleman and lived in a castle and that God's angels spoke to him, she told the others. They all laughed and said he was as crazy as his grandfather.

Hans ran home, hid in the corner, and cried.

*Now they knew she was a real princess,*
*for she was so sensitive, she had felt the pea*
*through twenty mattresses and twenty eiderdown quilts.*

*—from* THE PRINCESS AND THE PEA

When Hans was seven, his parents took him to see a play at the local theater. He was so thrilled by it, even though it was in German, that he decided then and there he was destined to be an actor. After that, he would sit for hours in front of a mirror with his mother's apron over his shoulders, pretending it was a knight's cloak. He would recite lines from any plays he had seen or read.

He began to write things, too, and soon considered himself a *digter*, which is the Danish word for *poet* or *author*.

Some of his neighbors thought him a pest, for he bothered all the people he knew to let him read his pieces aloud to them.

Others thought he was going mad, like his grandfather.

But a few thought he was—quite possibly—a genius, and they encouraged him, opening their houses to the little *digter*.

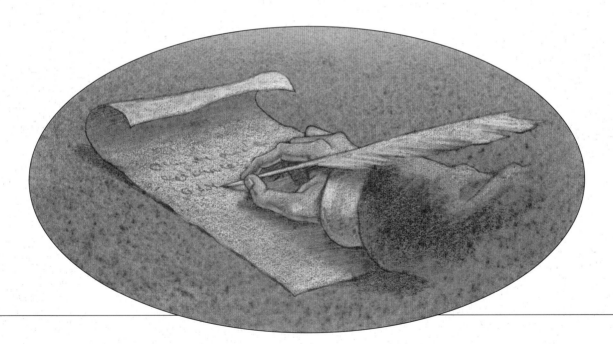

*"When you are given a good idea,*
*you should never let it go," Godfather said. "I went home*
*straightaway and made this book for you."*
—*from* GODFATHER'S PICTURE BOOK

His beloved father fell ill when Hans was only eleven.

Sent by his mother to fetch help, Hans ran to a so-called "wisewoman" a few miles from their house. The wisewoman made strange signs over him and told him to walk home by the riverbank. "If your father is to die," she said, "you will meet his ghost."

Hans met nothing along the way, but three days later, his father lay dead on the bed anyway.

"The Ice Maiden has taken him," Hans' mother said.

Because of his father's death, his mother had to leave Hans entirely alone and go out to wash other people's laundry all day so they would have enough money for food.

Hans kept writing his little poems and stories and plays, but death often came into his stories now.

*This is the home of the Ice Maiden,*
*who kills all that come near her. She can sail on a twig*
*down a great river, or leap from cliff to cliff with her snow-white hair*
*and her blue-green dress streaming behind her.*

—*from* THE ICE MAIDEN

At thirteen, Hans sneaked into the Odense theater through the backstage door because he had no money for tickets. Once inside, he told all of the actors how much he loved the theater. They found him amusing and arranged for him to have a tiny part in the operetta *Cendrillon*. He was thrilled. Not only did he have a line to say, he got to wear a red silk costume. He was certain that he would soon be known throughout Denmark.

Having read about famous men who had been born into humble homes, Hans told his mother, "First you go through terrible suffering, and then you become famous."

Hans grew into a gawky, long-legged lad. Often he wore a shabby grey coat, the sleeves of which did not reach as far as his thin wrists. Around his long neck he wound a calico scarf. He had small almond-shaped eyes, a big nose, and thick golden hair.

He was a stork among pigeons.

A cuckoo in the nest.

An ugly cygnet in a hatch of ducks.

*At last the big egg cracked open. "Peep . . . peep,"*
*said the ugly duckling as he tumbled out. "Why, none of the others*
*look a bit like that," said Mother Duck. "He shall have to go*
*into the water if I have to kick him in myself!"*

—*from* THE UGLY DUCKLING

When he was fourteen, it was time for Hans to learn a trade. His mother wanted him apprenticed to a bookbinder or a tailor—good, respectable work.

Hans wept at the thought. He wanted to become an actor in the capital city, Copenhagen. "My entire soul was burning for this art," he wrote.

So his mother begged the mail-coach driver to let her son ride for six shillings to the outskirts of Copenhagen. Clutching a small bundle of his clothes, he walked from there into the city.

What a big place it was, bustling with people: men and women and children, but no one in the whole place that he knew.

He was fourteen years old and entirely on his own.

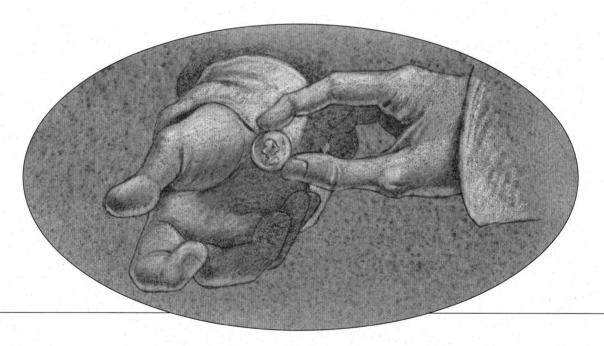

*There was once a silver shilling freshly minted.*
*My, how he jumped and jingled and cried,*
*"Huzzah! I'm off to see the great wide world!"*
*And off he went.*
—*from* THE SILVER SHILLING

The very next day, Hans went to call on the Royal Theater's leading ballerina at her home. He wore his best clothes, which were only slightly wrinkled from being in the bundle. On his head was a hat so big, it almost covered his eyes. He wore new boots with the pants tucked inside. What a sight!

Carrying a letter of introduction from an Odense printer, he knocked on the ballerina's door. Once inside, he gave her the note. She had never heard of the printer. Or of Hans.

Hoping to impress her, Hans began to sing and dance in his stocking feet, using the hat as a tambourine. She had him thrown out.

So he went on to the theater, but the manager advised him to go home.

*"I wonder how they're getting on with their work,"*
*thought the Emperor. He felt unwell when he remembered*
*that anyone stupid or unfit for office would never see what was woven.*
*Not that he'd any fears about himself.*

—*from* THE EMPEROR'S NEW CLOTHES

But Hans refused to go home. It was not in him to give up so quickly. After all, he wanted to become a famous man. He was prepared for some suffering.

A few good folk of Copenhagen, whom he had met through friends, took pity on him. Believing he really did have a core of genius, they gave him money to live on and sent him to the theater's ballet school. As a member of the ballet school, he received a small salary, plus shoes and stockings.

A well-known singer gave Hans singing lessons. He took acting lessons as well. He wanted to play the hero in every theater production, but the acting teacher said, "Your appearance is against you. People would only laugh at such a lanky hero."

Then Hans got his first role. He played a troll in the ballet *Armida*.

Hans was so thrilled, he took the program to bed with him, where in the candlelight he stared blissfully at his name. He thought it had "a halo of immortality about it."

*There was once a darning needle who was so fine,*
*she fancied she was a sewing needle.*

—*from* THE DARNING NEEDLE

Now established in the theater company—or so he thought—Hans turned his hand once again to writing.

He had very little money. Often he went all day without a hot meal. He spent lunchtime in the Copenhagen parks, which were lovely in the spring and summer. But in the winter—because he had no overcoat, and his boots were broken down—he was bitterly cold.

His room was so small that if he wanted to read or write, he had to sit on the bed.

There, by candlelight, he wrote poems and stories and plays, which he read aloud to anyone who would listen.

*There was once a young man who was studying
to be an author. He wanted to become one before Easter.
He thought it would be an easy life—if only he could find something
to write about, but alas, no ideas came to him.*

—*from* A QUESTION OF IMAGINATION

At first much of what Hans wrote seemed copied from works he loved. When a woman friend pointed this out to him, he cried, "Yes, I know, but aren't they wonderful!"

He took several plays to the Royal Theater, including one called *The Robbers of Vissenberg*. Not only did the directors reject the plays, but they dismissed him from the theater company as well. They had had enough of the annoying, awkward boy who could not stop telling everyone about his own genius.

But Hans was so fired up by his own writing, he could not stop working at it. Soon a scene from his play was printed in a small magazine.

A few months later, he paid to have his first book published. (This was not unusual in Andersen's time.) He wrote the book under the name Villiam Christian Walter—*Villiam* for William Shakespeare and *Walter* for Sir Walter Scott, his favorite authors. The book was so unsuccessful, most of the pages ended up being sold for wrapping paper.

*The student stood lost in reading
from the sheet of paper that the cheese had been wrapped in.
It was a page ripped from an old, unwanted book that should never have been
torn like that, for it was a wonderful book full of poetry.*

—*from* THE GOBLIN AT THE GROCER'S

Poor Hans. No money, no fame, his first book so poorly received it was used to wrap cheese.

This could have been the end of the story.

It could have read: "Defeated, the poor, ugly shoemaker's son returned home to Odense to become a street sweeper."

But strangely, the directors of the Royal Theater suddenly changed their minds. Perhaps it was the play excerpt in the magazine, or the publication of his book. Perhaps they finally saw that spark of genius in Hans. Perhaps they were afraid that if Hans really did become a famous writer, they would be laughed at. Or perhaps they admired the fact that he just never gave up.

Whatever the reason, they paid for Hans to go off to a grammar school to be properly educated. Imagine the tall, gawky seventeen-year-old Hans in a classroom with eleven-year-olds. The history master said of him, "One could cut him in half and make two puppies out of him."

*The three brothers were sent off to school,*
*and one became head of the class, one was square in the middle,*
*and the third was the dunce—which doesn't, of course, mean that they*
*weren't all equally clever and equally good.*

—*from* PEITER, PETER, AND PEER

That first year at the university, Hans was twenty-three years old. In January, he paid for the publication of his second book, *The Journey on Foot from Holmens Canal to the East Point of Amager*. It is a fantasy in which a young poet time-travels to the year 2129, meeting aliens, Saint Peter, and a king with hundred-league boots. It was a great success.

Later that year, he wrote a mock heroic play, *Love in Saint Nicolas' Tower*. It was produced at the Royal Theater, which had thrown him out six years earlier.

After the performance, Hans ran to the house of a friend. He threw himself into a chair, crying hysterically. His friend's wife, thinking to comfort him, said, "Don't take it to heart, Hans. Many great writers have been hissed off the stage."

"But they didn't hiss at all," he told her, still sobbing. "They applauded and shouted, 'Long live the *digter!* Long live the author!'"

In 1834, when he was just turning thirty, Hans began writing a book of fairy tales— *eventyrs*—for children. There were only four stories in the book: "The Tinder Box," "The Princess and the Pea," "Little Claus and Big Claus," and "Little Ida's Flowers." He paid for the book to be published in the spring of 1835, writing to a friend, "People will say this is my immortal work!" How right he was. By December of the same year, he published a second book of fairy tales, among them the ever-popular "Thumbelina." Suddenly he was famous, both in Denmark and in the rest of Europe as well. A swan among the ducks.

*"I shall never forget that the very first time I sang for you, you wept, and to a poet's heart, such tears are jewels."*

—*from* THE NIGHTINGALE

Hans went on to write over 150 fairy tales, including "The Little Mermaid," "The Ugly Duckling," "The Nightingale," and "The Snow Queen." Taking many of the old stories and superstitions his mother had taught him, he blended them with the books his father had read him, the plays he had seen, the literature and the poetry he adored. He put in scenes and landscapes from his life.

His children's stories allowed him to travel the world, dine with kings, become friends with famous people like the Brothers Grimm and Charles Dickens. While he never had any children of his own—for he never married—children all over the world owed their dreams to this perfect wizard.

After he died, at age seventy, in 1875, his fairy tales went on to be printed in dozens of languages. They have been made into movies, ballets, television shows, books, ice revues, and stage musicals.

They will live happily ever after.

*"Good-bye," sang the swallow, and flew back to Denmark.*
*There it had a little nest right above the window where the man lives*
*who tells fairy tales. The swallow sang to him for a day and a night.*
*And that's where this story comes from.*

—*from* THUMBELINA

*The passages that appear in the borders of this book are all from Andersen's fairy tales.*
*They were written and published during a thirty-five-year period.*
*The following dates indicate when the stories were published.*

1835
THE PRINCESS AND THE PEA

THUMBELINA

—◆—

1837
THE EMPEROR'S NEW CLOTHES

—◆—

1838
THE FLYING TRUNK

THE GARDEN OF EDEN

—◆—

1844
THE NIGHTINGALE

THE UGLY DUCKLING

—◆—

1845
THE FIR TREE

—◆—

1846
THE DARNING NEEDLE

—◆—

1851
THE PUPPET-SHOW MAN

—◆—

1853
THE GOBLIN AT THE GROCER'S

—◆—

1860
THE PEN AND THE INKWELL

—◆—

1861
WHAT FATHER DOES IS ALWAYS RIGHT

THE ICE MAIDEN

—◆—

1862
THE SILVER SHILLING

—◆—

1865
"THE WILL-O'-THE-WISPS ARE IN
TOWN," SAID THE BOG WITCH

—◆—

1868
GODFATHER'S PICTURE BOOK

PEITER, PETER, AND PEER

—◆—

1869
LUCK CAN BE FOUND IN A STICK

A QUESTION OF IMAGINATION

THE RAGS

*So you see, good can come even out of old rags,*
*once they leave the rag heap and are transformed into paper*
*on which truth and beauty are written.*

—*from* THE RAGS